First Trip to the Zoo

PAGE PUBLISHING, INC.
New York, NY

First originally published by Page Publishing, Inc. 2018

ISBN 978-1-64138-541-1 (Paperback)
ISBN 978-1-64138-542-8 (Digital)

Printed in the United States of America

First Trip to the Zoo

OLIVIA SHAFFER

On your first trip to the zoo,
The lions you will see.
With tigers, they are lurking,
Looking at you curiously.

Did you see the slow tortoise
On your way through the gate?
He'll be in the same spot
When you leave this great place.

On your first trip to the zoo,
Giraffes pick leaves
From the tallest of trees.

And the gorilla—he sits
and smiles happily.

On your first trip to the zoo,
Flamingos dance in the water.
Elephants hose off their backs
As the day gets hotter.

The brown bear will sleep.

The zebra will neigh.

13

The hippopotamus will swim
For most of the day.

On your first trip to the zoo,
The peacock roams free.
He struts his beautiful colors,
Waving his tail graciously.

The most ancient of creatures—
The crocodile—sunbathes
Until he sneaks in the water,
Barely making a wave.

Find a bench and have a snack,
But don't feed the pigeons.
They don't live at the zoo
But just came for a visit.

20

POLAR BEAR

Oh, look! The polar bear
Is always at play,
While the penguins will waddle
To get on their way.

They shimmy side to side
To climb up the rock.
Their keepers have built them a slide.
There they go! *Flop*!

The zoo is now closing.
The animals rest for the day.
As you head down the path,
Say goodbye and wave.

24

On your way home from the zoo,
Think of each creature
And what you can do
To protect Mother Nature.

About the Author

Olivia Shaffer was born and raised in Pennsylvania. She lives with her husband on their farm in Sinking Spring, with their dog and other farm animals. She enjoys gardening, horseback riding, and simple days on the countryside. Olivia is inspired by nature, music, and her childhood memories traveling the back roads of Lancaster County.

CPSIA information can be obtained
at www.ICGtesting.com
Printed in the USA
BVHW02s0632190618
519331BV00015B/48/P

9 781641 385411